FOCUS ON ENDANGERED SPECIES

ENDANGERED SHARKS

by Sue Gagliardi

BrightPoint Press

San Diego, CA

an imprint of ReferencePoint Press, Inc.
Printed in the United States

For more information, contact:
BrightPoint Press
PO Box 27779
San Diego, CA 92198
www.BrightPointPress.com

LIBRARY OF CONGRESS CATALOGING-IN-PUBLICATION DATA

Names: Gagliardi, Sue, 1969--author.
Title: Endangered sharks / by Sue Gagliardi.
Description: San Diego, CA: BrightPoint Press, [2024] | Series: Focus on endangered species | Includes bibliographical references and index. | Audience: Ages 13 | Audience: Grades 7-9
Identifiers: LCCN 2023004122 (print) | LCCN 2023004123 (eBook) | ISBN 9781678206482 (hardcover) | ISBN 9781678206499 (eBook)
Subjects: LCSH: Sharks--Conservation--Juvenile literature.
Classification: LCC QL638.9 .G224 2024 (print) | LCC QL638.9 (eBook) | DDC 597.3--dc23/eng/20230313
LC record available at https://lccn.loc.gov/2023004122
LC eBook record available at https://lccn.loc.gov/2023004123

CONTENTS

AT A GLANCE

- Many shark species are endangered due to human activity.
- Mako sharks are the fastest sharks in the world. Shark finning poses a major threat to this species.
- Some groups propose banning shark finning. Others work to regulate which species can be killed.
- Whale sharks are the biggest sharks in the world. They are especially vulnerable to injuries from plastic pollution. Large pieces can kill them. Small pieces, called microplastics, can poison them.
- Some people hold beach cleanups to get rid of pollution before it breaks down in the sea. Others, like the Ocean Cleanup, are tackling the large amount of trash already in the water.
- Great hammerhead sharks get their name from their hammer-shaped heads. Their head shape makes them more likely to get caught in shark meshing nets.

- New technology means that shark meshing can be done more safely. Some nets have alarms in them to warn animals to stay away.

- Zebra sharks live in coral reefs. Coral reefs provide them with food, protection, and a place to lay their eggs. These habitats are threatened by global warming and pollution.

- Chemicals such as herbicides and fertilizers can kill coral. Rain can wash these chemicals into waterways that lead to the ocean. People can protect coral reefs by limiting the use of these dangerous chemicals.

INTRODUCTION

A CLOSE CALL

A whale shark swims off the coast of Australia. It's early spring. The whale shark is making its yearly **migration**. Its large, speckled body glides near the surface of the water. It sees a school of small fish ahead. The whale shark opens its mouth to drag the fish in. It doesn't notice the fishing ships above.

One of the ships lowers its net as the whale shark swims by. The shark becomes tangled in the net. Other fish are caught in

Whale sharks move very slowly. Their top speed is about 4 miles per hour (6 kmh).

the net too. The whale shark thrashes its huge body from side to side. It struggles to break free. The fishers start to raise their net. Just as the net breeches the water, the whale shark's weight snaps one of the lines. It swims away, dragging the net behind it. The shark eventually shakes off the heavy lines. The whale shark is safe for now. But the threat of capture continues to be part of the shark's daily life.

SHARKS IN DANGER

Not all sharks are as lucky as this whale shark. Millions of sharks are killed by people

Only about 10 percent of whale sharks survive to adulthood.

every year. Sometimes the sharks are killed on purpose. Other times they're killed accidentally. Many sharks are hunted and captured for their meat, oil, and fins. The oil is made into medicine. The fins and meat are used in different foods.

Sharks can also be caught as bycatch. This means the sharks were caught by accident when people were trying to catch different fish. Other sharks are killed by boats. Still others are killed by pollution. These dangers are causing many shark populations to decline. Some species may go **extinct** if more isn't done to protect them. **Conservationists** are working to save these amazing animals.

More than one in three shark species are threatened with extinction.

1

SHORTFIN MAKO SHARKS

Shortfin mako sharks are one of two types of mako sharks. Their back fins are much shorter than the longfin mako sharks'. Shortfin makos have pointed snouts and long gill slits. They have dark blue-and-gray backs. Their undersides are white. Fully grown shortfin mako sharks can measure up to 12 feet (3.7 m) long. They can weigh more than 1,200 pounds (540 kg). They can live more than thirty years.

Female shortfin mako sharks give birth to live pups. The pups are about 2 feet (0.6 m) long when they're born. Their large size protects them

The shortfin mako shark is one of only five warm-blooded shark species.

The shortfin mako shark gets its name from the Indigenous people of Polynesia. The Maori people's word for shark is mako.

from predators. Young shortfin mako sharks live in coastal waters. Adults live farther offshore.

Shortfin makos are the world's fastest sharks. They can swim up to 45 miles per hour (72 kmh). This helps them migrate long distances. They can travel across entire oceans.

There are two types of shortfin mako sharks. Atlantic shortfin makos live in the Atlantic Ocean. Pacific shortfin makos are found in the Pacific Ocean. Atlantic shortfin mako populations are decreasing particularly rapidly.

THREATS TO SHORTFIN MAKO SHARKS

People kill more than 1 million shortfin mako sharks each year. They are hunted for their

Shark fins are worth up to $500 per pound ($1,100 per kg). They are used to make shark fin soup.

meat and fins. One of the major threats to shortfin mako sharks is the shark finning trade. Their fins are used to make shark fin soup.

Many shark advocates describe shark finning as cruel. Fishers first catch sharks. They then cut off their fins. The rest of the shark is thrown back into the ocean. The sharks are still alive when they're thrown back. But they can't survive without their fins. They die slowly. Some drown. They need to move for their gills to work. Others bleed to death. Sometimes the shark becomes prey for other sharks because it cannot swim away from danger.

SHARK FIN SOUP

Shark fin soup is a symbol of wealth and power in some parts of Asia. It is a traditional soup that dates back 2,000 years. Some organizations suggest new ways of making the soup without using real shark fins. But many people are slow to make this change.

Even in places where shark finning is banned, poachers and smugglers continue the trade.

Researchers examined scraps from nearly 10,000 shark fins from fish markets in Hong Kong, China. The researchers took **DNA** from the shark fins. They used it to determine which species the fins belonged to. They found eighty-six different species of sharks in the shark fin samples. More than 70 percent of the species sampled were at risk of extinction. Mako sharks are just one of these species.

Shark finning is a major reason for the decrease in shark populations. As many as 100 million sharks are killed every year due to shark finning. Shark finning is unsustainable. It causes shark populations to decrease rapidly. Mako sharks are no exception. They have lost 99.9 percent of their population since the 1700s.

Shark finning is particularly harmful to species that don't reproduce quickly.

HOW BIG IS A SHARK?

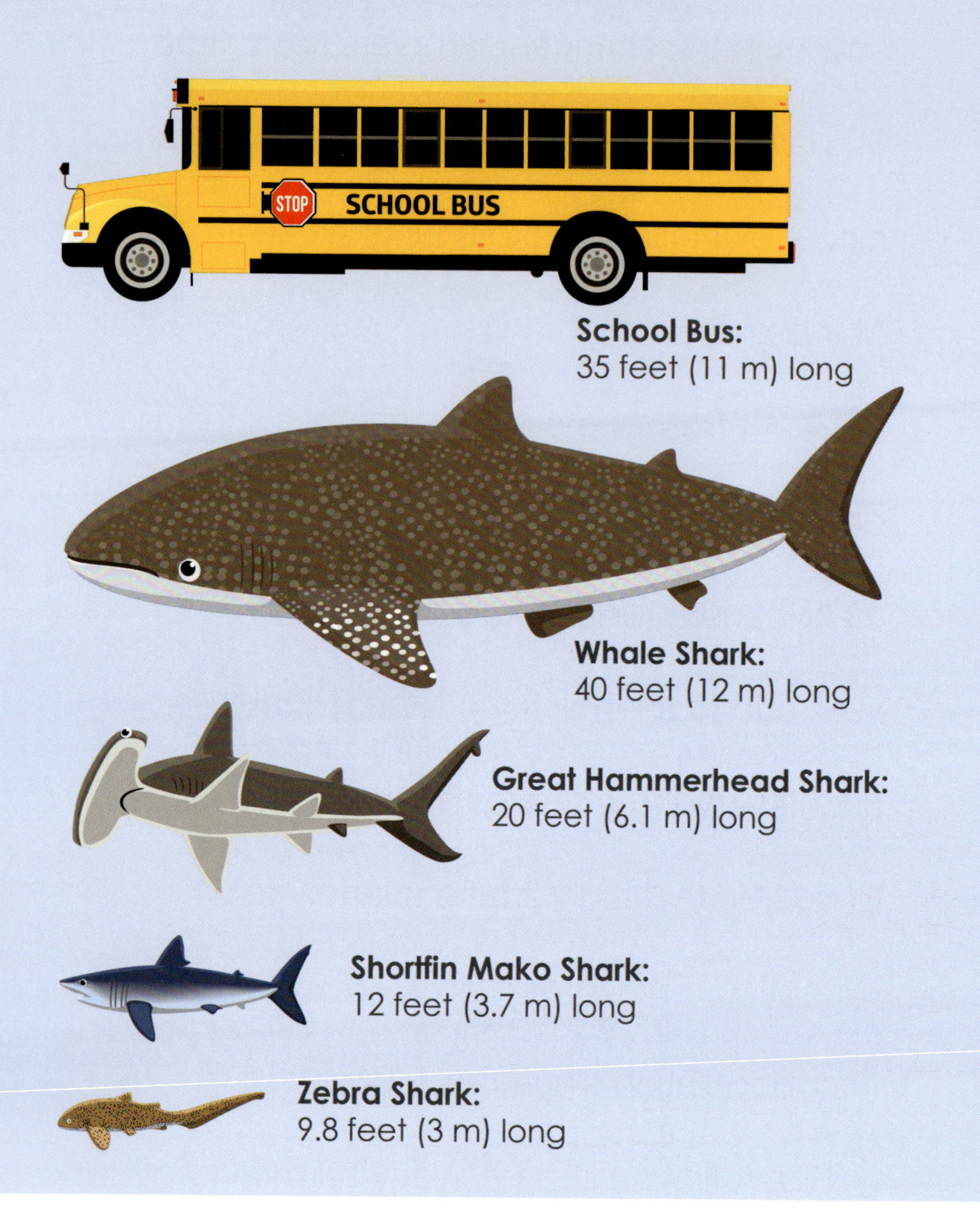

Sharks come in many different sizes.

Shortfin mako sharks are one such species. Male Atlantic shortfin mako sharks can't reproduce until they're eight years old. Females must wait longer. They can't have babies until they're nineteen years old. Their pregnancy is long too. Shortfin mako sharks are pregnant for eighteen months before they give birth. They can give birth only once every three years. These factors make it hard for their population to recover.

CONSERVATION EFFORTS

Many organizations work to protect mako sharks through conservation. Researchers at the Shark Research Institute are working to end shark finning. They are helping to pass laws that ban this practice. Shark finning is banned in some US states. But shark finning continues worldwide.

Other organizations work specifically to save shortfin mako sharks. The National Oceanic and Atmospheric Administration

THE FINS-ATTACHED METHOD

Fins-attached fishing rules help limit the number of sharks killed for their fins. Under this system, fishers must bring the whole shark back to land with its fins attached. This limits the number of sharks a fishing vessel can catch. Whole sharks take up more room than shark fins.

(NOAA) is one such organization. In 2022, NOAA banned US fishers from hunting or selling any Atlantic shortfin mako sharks.

Many believe the government should do more to help these sharks. Jane Davenport is an attorney who works to protect endangered species. She says, "The shortfin mako shark is the world's fastest-swimming shark, but it can't outrace the threat of extinction. The government must follow the science and provide much-needed federal protections as quickly as possible."[1]

2

WHALE SHARKS

Whale sharks are the largest species of shark. They can measure more than 40 feet (12 m) long. That's longer than most school buses. They weigh about 30,000 pounds (14,000 kg). These sharks also have long lives. They can live up to 150 years in the wild.

Whale sharks have blue-gray bodies. Their undersides are pale. They have distinct patterns of white stripes and spots on their backs. Their patterns help them blend into their environment.

Whale sharks can have more than 1,000 animals living in their huge mouths. Tiny shrimplike creatures find protection and food in the sharks' mouths.

Whale sharks have big mouths to match their big bodies. They have more than 3,000 small teeth in more than 300 rows. But they do not bite or chew their food. Whale sharks are filter feeders. They swim with their mouths open and suck

WHALE SHARKS ARE NOT WHALES

Though whale sharks are as big as some whales, they are different animals. Whales are mammals. Whale sharks are fish. They breathe underwater using gills. Whales surface to breathe using their lungs. Whale sharks have skeletons made of cartilage. Whales have skeletons made of bone.

up the water in their path. Their gills filter out the water and leave prey behind.

The sharks mainly catch plankton and tiny fish. Their gills filter more than 1,600 gallons (6,000 L) of water every hour. Using this process, even a young whale shark can capture about 46 pounds (21 kg) of plankton every day.

Whale sharks live in warm waters. They are found throughout the Indian Ocean. They travel thousands of miles each spring as they migrate to the coast of Australia.

THREATS TO WHALE SHARKS

Whale sharks have few known predators in the sea. Most threats to whale sharks come from human activity. Whale sharks swim at a slow speed near the surface of the water. This makes them easy to capture and kill. Whale sharks are hunted for their liver oil and fins.

Boats are some of the biggest threats to whale sharks. Many busy shipping routes go through waters where whale sharks are found. Large boats can strike and kill whale sharks. The animals can be injured by a ship's propellers.

Between 6,000 and 8,000 whale sharks are killed by humans every year.

Pollution is another danger that whale sharks face. Whale sharks take in thousands of gallons of water every day. Hidden in the water are dangerous microplastics. Plastic pollution doesn't break down the way that organic matter does. It instead is torn into thousands of

Plastic pollution kills 100,000 marine mammals and sea turtles and 1 million sea birds every year.

tiny pieces. Pieces smaller than 3/16 of an inch (5 mm) are called microplastics.

Elitza Germanov researches marine animals. She says, “Filter feeders might accidentally scoop up [microplastics] because they float among their prey.”[2] Germanov says that whale sharks may be ingesting as many as 137 pieces of plastic every hour.

Five millimeters isn't very big. It's about the size of a pencil eraser. But microplastics are very dangerous. They can expose animals to poisonous chemicals. These chemicals can hurt the animals' growth. They can also make it more difficult for the animals to have babies. Larger plastic pieces are dangerous too. The pieces can get stuck in the creatures' digestive tracts. This can injure or kill the animals.

This plastic problem is growing. Plastic production is increasing. A lot of it will eventually become pollution. In 2021, 10 percent of all waste plastic ended up in the ocean. That's 10 million tons (9 million metric tons) of plastic every year.

SAVING WHALE SHARKS

One way people are saving whale sharks is by reducing ship speed limits. Others propose changing shipping routes to avoid whale shark migration paths. People hope these efforts will prevent ship strikes.

Whale sharks are protected under the International Convention on Migratory Species. They are also protected by

One way that scientists save whale sharks is through rehabilitation. This baby whale shark was rescued from a net and raised until it could live in the wild again.

Australia's Wildlife Conservation Act. These rules make it illegal for people to hurt whale sharks. But there are still places where fishing is **unregulated**. Whale sharks are in danger in these areas.

Despite the conservation work being done, whale shark populations are decreasing.

Scientists are tracking whale sharks to learn more about them. There are several ways to do this. One way is by using whale sharks' unique patterns of stripes and spots to tell them apart. Since 2007, scientists have been able to use this method to identify more than 450 individual whale sharks. Other conservationists use satellite tags to track whale sharks. These tags help researchers learn about the sharks' **habitat** and migration routes.

Education is also an important part of conservation. In Australia, researchers promote **ecotourism** to teach people about whale sharks. Tourists can swim with whale sharks and learn more about them.

Cleaning up the ocean is also important. One team working toward this is the Ocean Cleanup. The Ocean Cleanup uses special tools to take garbage out of the ocean. System 002 is one of these tools.

System 002 looks like a big net. It's pulled by two boats. The boats use computer systems to figure out where big patches of garbage are. The boats pull the net through the garbage. The net is then pulled on board and emptied. The garbage is taken back to land and recycled. In July 2022, the Ocean Cleanup announced that it had pulled more than 220,000 pounds (100,000 kg) of trash from the ocean. The group's goal is to remove 90 percent of the plastic from the ocean by 2040.

But people don't need special tools to make a difference. Some scientists say

System 002 is designed to protect marine animals. It has underwater cameras to watch for animals caught in the net.

that the best way to keep plastic out of the ocean is through beach cleanups. Picking up garbage from beaches stops plastic from breaking down in the water. This helps protect whale sharks and other marine life.

3
GREAT HAMMERHEAD SHARKS

The great hammerhead shark is the largest species of hammerhead. It can grow up to 20 feet (6.1 m) long. It can weigh up to 991 pounds (450 kg). These sharks get their name from their hammer-shaped heads. Their heads have electrical receptors that can sense prey. This allows them to find prey that is hidden in sand.

Great hammerheads have seventeen rows of teeth on their upper and lower jaws. Their teeth are long and serrated. They use

Great hammerhead sharks have few predators, but they may sometimes eat each other.

these sharp teeth to catch stingrays and squid.

Great hammerheads can live more than forty-four years in the wild. They start having babies at around five to nine years old. Great hammerheads give birth to six to forty-two pups at a time. They give birth once every two years.

These sharks have live young instead of laying eggs. Hammerheads give birth in shallow, coastal waters. Young hammerhead sharks live in these areas until they are large enough to move to deeper waters. The adult sharks don't stay with them. Great hammerheads are **solitary** sharks. They migrate up to 756 miles (1,220 km) each year by themselves.

THREATS TO HAMMERHEAD SHARKS

Hammerhead sharks are decreasing in number all over the world. Their population

SHARK'S-EYE VIEW

Hammerhead sharks can see with a 360-degree view. This is because their eyes are set on the ends of their hammer-shaped heads. This placement gives the sharks a wide range of vision. They can see above and below them at the same time. They also move their heads sideways as they swim. This helps them see what's behind them.

has declined by more than 80 percent over the past seventy years. Hammerhead sharks are endangered due to commercial fishing and accidental catches. They are also threatened by the shark fin trade.

Shark meshing is another major threat to hammerhead sharks. Shark meshing is when people place nets in the waters along coastlines. These nets are designed to keep sharks away from swimmers. But these nets can be dangerous. Sharks can get tangled in these nets when they swim close to shore. They often drown when they cannot break free. Hammerhead sharks are

Great hammerheads need to be moving for their gills to work. They can drown if they get trapped in a net.

especially likely to get caught in these nets due to the unique shape of their heads.

Shark meshing might seem like a good idea. But it isn't clear if this practice really protects people. The nets don't stretch along the full beach. This means they cannot reliably keep sharks away from people.

PROTECTING HAMMERHEADS

Some new shark meshing nets are designed with the goal of protecting both sea life and humans. Some are fitted with alarms to keep marine animals away. This can stop sharks from becoming trapped.

The Center for Biological Diversity is also working to protect great hammerhead sharks. In 2022, this organization started a petition to protect hammerhead sharks

Workers in New South Wales check shark nets every three days to free any marine life that may be trapped.

under the Endangered Species Act. This would make it illegal to hurt great hammerheads in the United States. It would also ban selling hammerhead shark parts in the United States, even if the sharks were caught somewhere else. The petition pointed out that great hammerheads are

Over the last seventy years, great hammerhead shark populations have declined by 80 percent.

already listed as critically endangered by the International Union for Conservation of Nature. They argued that great hammerheads could become extinct in the wild if they do not get protection soon.

Emily Jeffers is an attorney with the Center for Biological Diversity. “These huge animals desperately need federal help,” Jeffers says. “With Endangered Species Act protections, we can ensure the next generation will see these amazing creatures in the wild. Great hammerheads won’t be around much longer unless we act now.”[3]

Despite their pleas, the government wasn’t convinced. After reviewing the petition, it said there wasn’t enough evidence that great hammerheads were in danger. The petition was denied.

4

ZEBRA SHARKS

Zebra sharks get their name from the white stripes they're born with. These stripes fade as the sharks grow older. Adult zebra sharks look very different from their pups. The adults are tan with dark spots.

Zebra sharks are found in the tropical waters of the western Pacific and

Indian Oceans. They can grow up to 9.8 feet (3 m) long. But they weigh only up to 66 pounds (30 kg). Their tails are about as long as their bodies. They can live between twenty-five and thirty years in the wild.

Zebra sharks have fleshy organs on their snouts called barbels. The sharks use them to find food.

These sharks are nocturnal. They hunt for prey at night. They spend the day resting near coral reefs on the ocean floor.

Zebra sharks do not give birth to live pups. They instead lay eggs. Zebra sharks lay their eggs on rocks in coral reefs. The growing shark is protected by an egg case. These egg cases are nicknamed mermaid purses. They are purple and brown. They're also big. These egg cases are about 6.7 inches (17 cm) long. The egg cases grow as the baby sharks develop. It takes about six and a half months for the eggs to hatch.

Each zebra shark egg is unique. Scientists can use its size and shape to figure out which female laid it.

THREATS TO ZEBRA SHARKS

Habitat destruction is one of the biggest threats facing zebra sharks. The coral reefs they call home are being destroyed by pollution. Oil, trash, and chemical waste are all dangerous to coral reefs.

Pollution is also killing coral reefs in another way. Air pollution from human activity is making the world hotter. This is called global warming. Global warming is one of the biggest dangers facing coral reefs.

Coral reefs normally have bright colors. These colors come from the algae that

SEARCHING FOR HIDDEN PREY

Zebra sharks are adapted to live in coral reefs. Their flexible bodies help them wiggle into narrow cracks and channels in the reefs. They move with eellike motions. The sharks search for hidden prey in the reefs. They suck up their prey with their small mouths and gill muscles.

In 2022, 91 percent of the reefs surveyed in the Great Barrier Reef were impacted by coral bleaching.

live within the coral. When the ocean water warms as little as 2 degrees Fahrenheit (1°C), the algae may leave the coral. The coral turns white. This is called coral bleaching. It eventually kills the coral. This can be deadly to zebra sharks.

Oceanographer Nicole Couto says, "Sharks are important to coral reefs and coral reefs are important to sharks, so one can only be healthy if the other is."[4] Couto explains that coral reefs provide sharks with food and protection from predators. Reefs also provide habitats for baby sharks. Sharks are important to the coral too. They remove fish that carry disease.

BOTTOM DWELLERS

Zebra sharks are bottom-dwelling sharks. They spend their days swimming on the ocean floor near coral reefs. Their throat muscles pump water across their gills. This allows them to breathe while staying still.

PROTECTING THE REEF

One way to protect zebra sharks is to protect their coral reef homes. Some groups work to protect and regrow coral reefs. Other programs focus on the species itself. One initiative works with zoos to raise zebra sharks in captivity and then release them into the wild.

People can help protect coral reefs by avoiding the use of fertilizers, herbicides, and pesticides. These chemicals can run off into waterways that lead to the oceans. The chemicals pollute the oceans and harm ocean habitats.

Off the coast of southern Africa, scuba divers study zebra sharks. They track zebra sharks and collect data about their coral reef habitats. Shark researcher Anna Flam says, "We should protect them. Otherwise, we could see them disappear."[5]

Sonja Fordham is the president of Shark Advocates International. She says, "Relatively simple safeguards can help to save sharks . . . but time is running out. We urgently need conservation action across the globe to . . . secure a brighter future for these extraordinary, irreplaceable animals."[6]

Zebra sharks are very friendly with humans. Some even let divers pet them.

GLOSSARY

conservationists

people who work toward the protection and preservation of natural environments, plants, and wildlife

DNA

deoxyribonucleic acid, a chemical in the cells of living things that stores genetic information

ecotourism

tourism that is focused on seeing wildlife and supporting conservation

extinct

no longer existing

habitat

the natural environment where an animal lives

migration

the movement from one place to another at certain times of the year

solitary

living or traveling alone

unregulated

having no rules or safety measures in place

SOURCE NOTES

CHAPTER ONE: SHORTFIN MAKO SHARKS

1. Quoted in "Lawsuit Launched over Federal Failure to Protect Shortfin Mako Shark," *Center for Biological Diversity*, June 28, 2022. https://biologicaldiversity.org.

CHAPTER TWO: WHALE SHARKS

2. Quoted in "Microplastics on the Menu for Manta Rays and Whale Sharks," *Marine Megafauna Foundation*, November 2, 2022. https://marinemegafauna.org.

CHAPTER THREE: GREAT HAMMERHEAD SHARKS

3. Quoted in Evan Noorani, "New Petition Aims to Protect Dwindling Great Hammerhead Shark Population from Extinction," *CBS8*, July 25, 2022. www.cbs8.com.

CHAPTER FOUR: ZEBRA SHARKS

4. Quoted in Nicole Couto, "How Badly Do Coral Reefs and Sharks Need Each Other?" *Oceanbites*, June 30, 2016. https://oceanbites.org.

5. Quoted in Nick and Caroline Robertson-Brown, "First Study of Zebra Sharks in Africa Reveals New Hotspot in Need of Protection," *Scubaverse*, July 14, 2021. www.scubaverse.com.

6. Quoted in Helen Briggs, "Extinction: 'Time Is Running Out' to Save Sharks and Rays," *BBC*, January 27, 2021. www.bbc.com.

FOR FURTHER RESEARCH

BOOKS

Elisa A. Bonnin, *Endangered Sharks*. San Diego, CA: BrightPoint Press, 2023.

Lisa Bullard, *We Need Sharks*. Lake Elmo, MN: Focus Readers, 2019.

Shark Attack. New York: DK Super Readers, 2023.

INTERNET SOURCES

"Sea Wonder: Zebra Sharks," *National Marine Sanctuary Foundation*, July 29, 2022. https://marinesanctuary.org.

Elizabeth Ward-Sing, "Great Hammerhead Shark," *Shark Guardian*, May 12, 2017. www.sharkguardian.org.

"Whale Shark," *National Geographic*, n.d. www.nationalgeographic.com.

WEBSITES

Conservation International

www.conservation.org

Conservation International works to protect and restore ecosystems. It currently protects land in more than seventy countries.

Sharks4Kids

www.sharks4kids.com

Sharks4Kids aims to educate children about sharks to create more advocates for marine life. It provides learning resources, games, and activities to help kids learn about sharks.

World Wildlife Fund

www.worldwildlife.org

The World Wildlife Fund was established in 1961. Today, the organization works in almost one hundred countries to help communities preserve natural resources.

INDEX

IMAGE CREDITS

Cover: © Derek Heasley/Shutterstock Images
5: © wildestanimal/Shutterstock Images
7: © Andrea Izzotti/Shutterstock Images
9: © Akhtar Soomro/Reuters/Alamy
11: © Tatiana Belova/Shutterstock Images
13: © Jessica Heim/Shutterstock Images
14: © Ryan Cake/iStockphoto
16: © 54613/Shutterstock Images
18: © Alessandro De Maddalena/Shutterstock Images
20 (sharks): © Bullet_Chained/iStockphoto
20 (bus): © Denis Dubrovin/Shutterstock Images
25: © Shane Myers Photography/Shutterstock Images
29: © Frolova_Elena/Shutterstock Images
30: © Rich Carey/Shutterstock Images
33: © Miss E Media/Shutterstock Images
34: © Filippo Bacci/iStockphoto
37: © The Ocean Cleanup
39: © Carlos Grillo/Shutterstock Images
43: © Carlos Grillo/Shutterstock Images
45: © John Carnemolla/Shutterstock Images
46: © Derek Heasley/Shutterstock Images
49: © Peter Lanzersdorfer/Shutterstock Images
51: © Tim Rock/Blue Planet Archive
53: © acro_phuket/Shutterstock Images
57: © Rich Carey/Shutterstock Images

ABOUT THE AUTHOR

Sue Gagliardi writes fiction, nonfiction, and poetry for children. She enjoys learning about sharks and ways to help protect them. She is a teacher and lives in Pennsylvania with her husband and son.